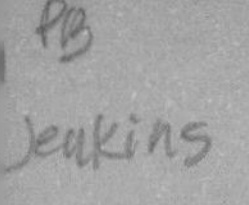

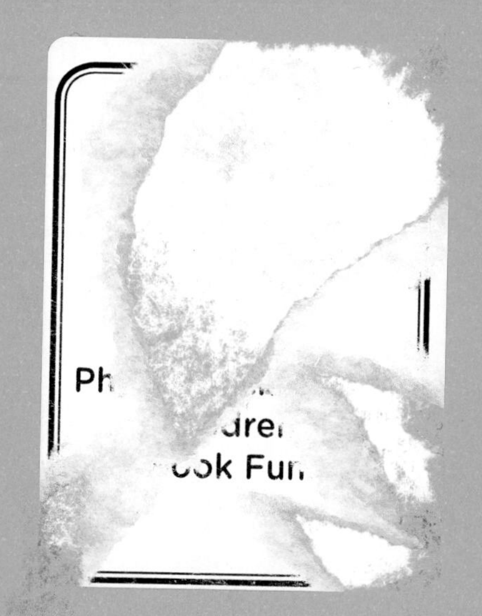

PRINCESSLAND

Emily Jenkins

PICTURES BY

Yoko Tanaka

FARRAR STRAUS GIROUX
New York

Romy didn't want to do anything.

Or make anything.

Or play with anybody.

Romy didn’t even want to be Romy, that day.

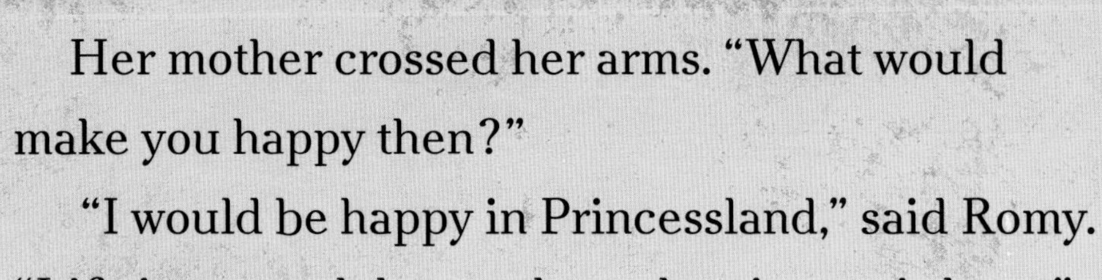

Her mother crossed her arms. "What would make you happy then?"

"I would be happy in Princessland," said Romy. "Life is so much better there than it ever is here."

Romy's mother sighed.

Romy sighed back.

On the porch, the Lady Cat woke from her morning nap. She stood and stretched, then meandered down the steps.

Romy followed.

“You’re in a bad mood,” said the Lady Cat eventually.

“Because it’s so boring here,” said Romy. “I wish I were in Princessland.”

“What’s it like in Princessland?”

“In Princessland,” said Romy, “all the girls are princesses.”

"Ah," said the Lady Cat, pausing to sniff a leaf on the sidewalk. "I could probably take you there, if you hang around long enough. Tell me more about it while we walk."

The Lady Cat headed straight for the bakery.

Romy followed.

They went around the back door and the baker gave Romy a day-old muffin. The Lady Cat got a dish of milk.

"In Princessland," said Romy, chewing, "there are good things to eat whenever you want them. Sandwiches of white bread and chocolate frosting. Raspberries and lollipops and cake."

The Lady Cat didn't reply, but turned her tail on Romy, the way cats do. She jumped

and jumped again

and jumped again.

Romy followed.

"In Princessland," continued Romy, "everyone lives in a castle with tall, tall towers and a moat full of alligators. They sleep in the highest rooms on beds of flower petals. They can look out their windows and see for miles."

“Sounds pretty,” said the cat.

“Oh, it’s beautiful.”

The Lady Cat leaped down. She headed for the town square at a trot.

Romy followed.

In the Saturday market, vendors sold fish, spices, pickles, jams, and hand-knit sweaters; bouquets of flowers and bright bolts of fabric. Romy and the Lady Cat dodged skirts and carts, weaving about until they reached the fish vendor, where the cat did something naughty, and then the ribbon seller, where Romy was given a strip of velvet that was too short for anyone to buy.

"In Princessland—Lady Cat, are you listening?—in Princessland, there are balls every night in enormous, airy rooms lined with marble tiles. The princesses wear satin slippers and gowns trimmed with pansies and lace."

"They dance to music from violins and harps and bells made of glass, with princes who never get tired or step on their feet."

The Lady Cat paid no attention. She left the market and headed to a patch of grass.

Romy followed.

"Lady Cat, where are you going?" Romy called. "Didn't you say you would take me to Princessland?"

"Excuse me," said the Lady Cat, crouching,

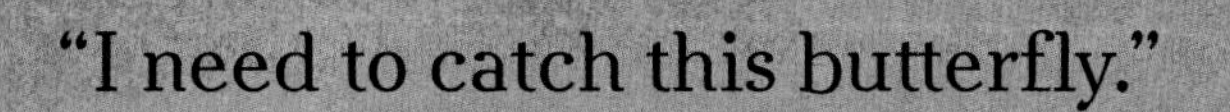

"I need to catch this butterfly."

"I haven't told you yet how each princess has a horse," Romy said. "A horse with the softest nose you could ever touch. Some of them also have lions they can ride. They meet talking animals and they battle dragons."

The Lady Cat missed catching her butterfly and then walked away all casual, pretending she never wanted it anyhow—the way cats do.

“At the end of the day,” said Romy, “the princesses lie on the banks of a sparkling river, cool their feet, and weave each other crowns of roses.”

The Lady Cat didn’t answer. She was asleep. Or something close to asleep, the way cats can be.

Romy pet her for a while.

The sun sank in the sky. They weren't far from home, and Romy heard her mother calling.

"I want my dinner," said the Lady Cat, lifting her head.

“Weren’t you going to take me to Princessland?” asked Romy.

“I did take you to Princessland,” said the Lady Cat.

“No you didn’t.”

“Ah, but I am sure I did.”

The Lady Cat trotted into the house.
Romy followed.

And when she thought about it, Romy understood that

the Lady Cat was right.

In memory of Frances Foster
—E.J.

For my mother, "P.R."
—Y.T.

Farrar Straus Giroux Books for Young Readers
An imprint of Macmillan Publishing Group, LLC
175 Fifth Avenue, New York 10010

Color separations by Bright Arts (H.K.) Ltd.
Printed in China by RR Donnelley Asia Printing Solutions Ltd.,
Dongguan City, Guangdong Province
Designed by Roberta Pressel
First edition, 2017
1 3 5 7 9 10 8 6 4 2

mackids.com

Library of Congress Cataloging-in-Publication Data

Names: Jenkins, Emily, 1967- author. | Tanaka, Yoko (Artist), illustrator.
Title: Princessland / Emily Jenkins ; pictures by Yoko Tanaka.
Description: First edition. | New York : Farrar Straus Giroux (BYR), 2017. |
Summary: Bored and in a bad mood, Romy wants Lady Cat to take her to Princessland, until Romy discovers that everyday life can be quite magical.
Identifiers: LCCN 2016024336 | ISBN 9780374361150 (hardback)
Subjects: | CYAC: Mood (Psychology)–Fiction. | Boredom–Fiction. | Princesses–Fiction. | Cats–Fiction. | BISAC: JUVENILE FICTION / Royalty. | JUVENILE FICTION / Humorous Stories.
Classification: LCC PZ7.J4134 Pr 2017 | DDC [E]–dc23
LC record available at https://lccn.loc.gov/2016024336